Puppy Book

By JAN PFLOOG

A GOLDEN BOOK • NEW YORK

Golden Books Publishing Company, Inc., New York, New York 10106

ISBN: 0-307-10078-2   MCMXCVII

Puppies come

in all sizes, shapes, and colors.

When they eat,

puppies are not very neat.

After eating, puppies like to have a drink.

Sometimes puppies chew on things
that are not for eating.

Puppies like to play
better than anything else.

They like to play tug-of-war.

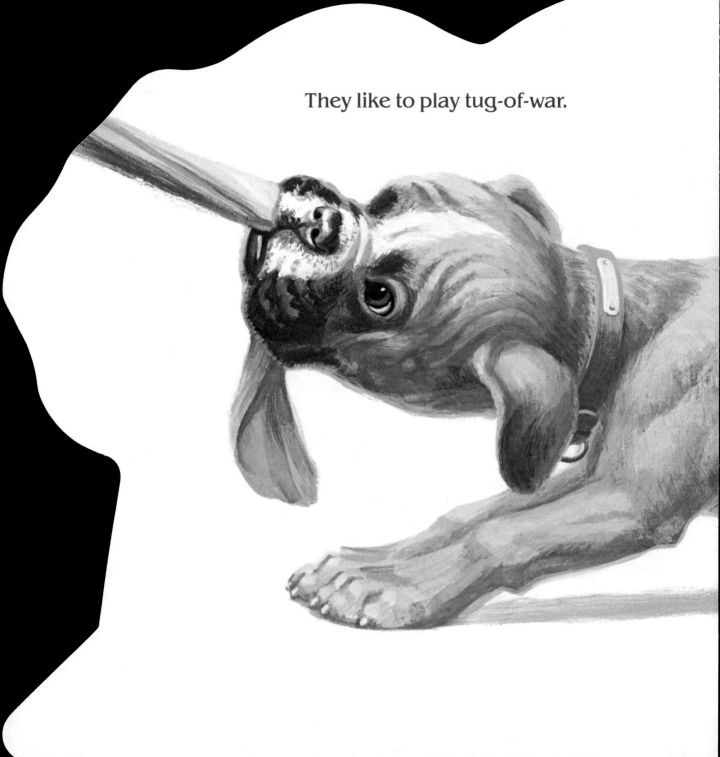

They like to chase a ball.

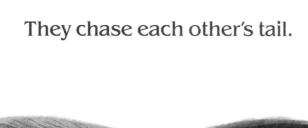

They chase each other's tail.

Sometimes they even chase their *own* tail!

Some puppies play with cats.

When puppies

get tired, they take a nap.

Sweet dreams, puppies.